Washington

# Henry the Explorer

## MARK TAYLOR

*illustrations by*

## GRAHAM BOOTH

Little, Brown and Company
Boston   Toronto

Library of Congress Catalog Card No. 88-81154

ISBN 0-316-83384-3

10  9  8  7  6  5  4  3  2  1

WOR

Published simultaneously in Canada
by Little, Brown & Company (Canada) Limited

Printed in the United States of America

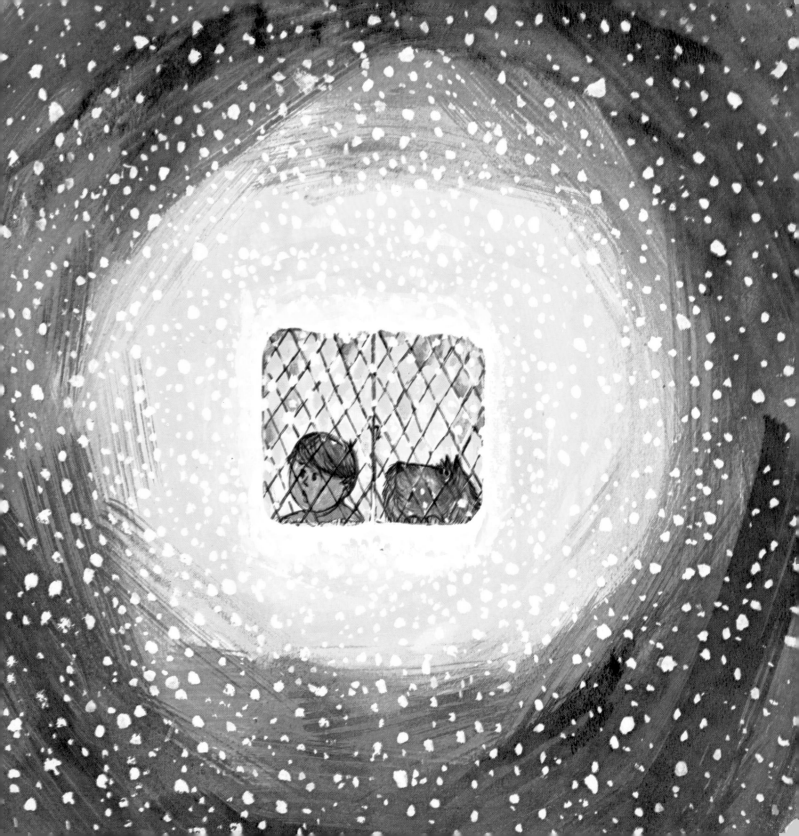

On the night of the blizzard,
Henry and Laird Angus McAngus
read an exciting book about exploring. So . . .

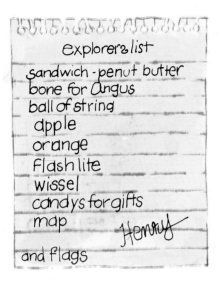

explorer's list

sandwich - penut butter
bone for Angus
ball of string
apple
orange
flash lite
wissel
candys for gifts
map
Henry
and flags

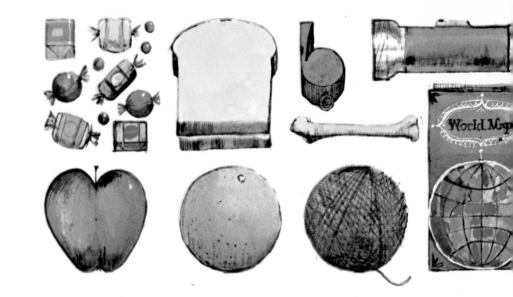

the next morning, after breakfast,
Henry got ready to go exploring. He carefully
made ready his explorer's kit. And he made
a great many flags in order to claim all the
wonderful things he planned to discover.

"Where are you and Angus going?" asked Henry's mother.

"Exploring," said Henry. "We will probably discover the whole world before we're through."

"Well, don't be late coming home," said his mother. "Try to finish exploring the world before it gets dark."

"All right—if a bear doesn't catch us," Henry replied.

"I wonder if there really are bears
out there, Angus," said Henry.

Henry discovered some friendly natives along the way.

He read his special speech claiming them.

Henry and Angus went farther and farther. They claimed
each great discovery with a flag.

Exploring made them very hungry.

Far from home, Henry discovered
a big dark forest.

And in the forest he discovered a cave!

"Careful, Angus! Don't wake up any bears."

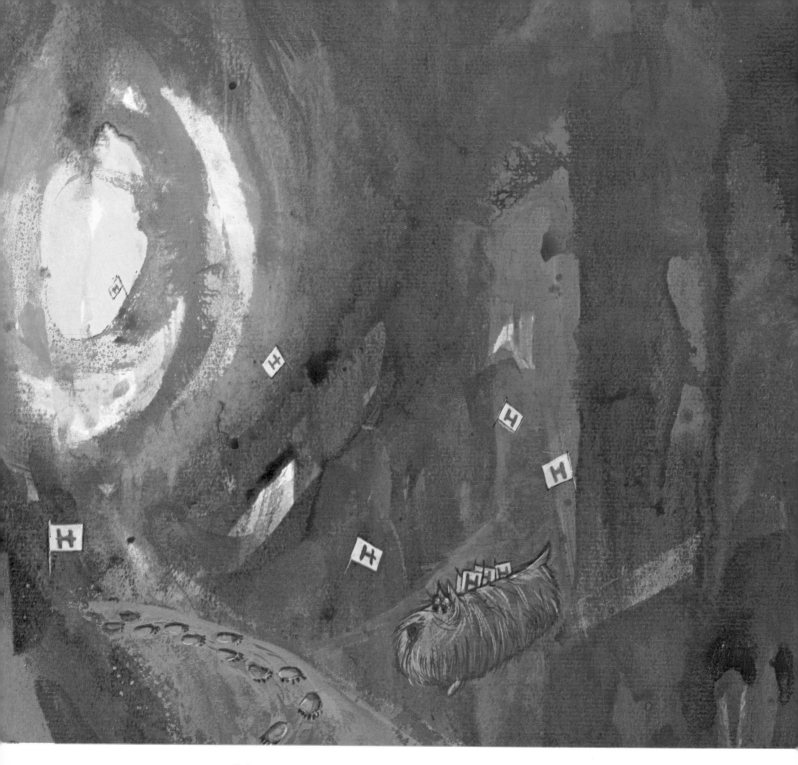

Of course, explorers must be very *very* careful in caves.
They have to avoid falling into pits, or getting lost.

And who knows what those lumpy things
among the shadows might be?

"What is that?" said Henry. "A bear!"

Then Henry knew it was time to leave.

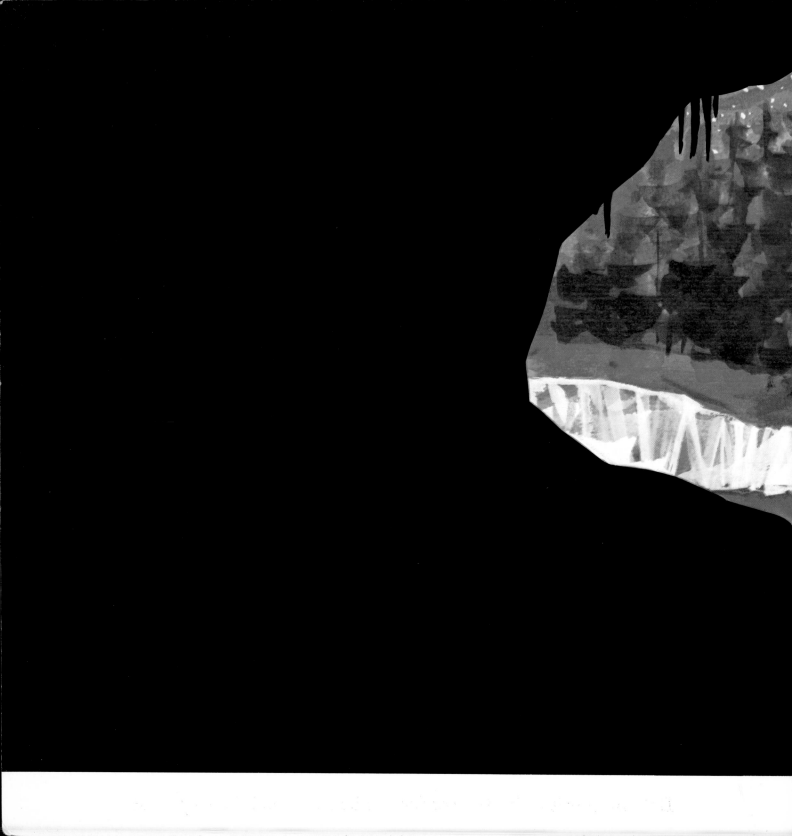

But now it was night. He wondered if he could find the way home.

When Henry had failed to come home by sundown,
his mother was so worried she called the neighbors.
The men organized a search.

"A good explorer can always find his way—
he just keeps looking," Henry told Angus.

Henry kept looking
for the way home.

The searchers kept looking
for Henry.

At last Henry found his own trail!

At last the searchers found Henry's footprints.

Now Henry knew home was not far away.

When she saw him, Henry's mother was overjoyed. "Henry!" she cried, "you have been found."

"I haven't been lost," said Henry. "But I did find a bear. Is supper ready?"

The searchers soon arrived, and they were glad to hear that Henry was safely home. "His trail led us right to the door," they said.

"Come in and have some coffee," said Henry's mother.

Henry said goodnight.

Henry was happy after a long day of exploring and meeting bears.

"This is a good book about jungles," he said. "I think we should explore the jungle next."

Angus thumped his tail in agreement.

"But first," said Henry . . .

". . . we'll have to make more flags."